Mind Your Manners, Biscuit!

by Alyssa Satin Capucilli

HarperFestival®
A Division of HarperCollins Publishers

"It's a beautiful day
for a walk, Biscuit."
Woof, woof!

"Mom has a list of errands, and we can help.
Let's go!"
Woof!

"We can mail a letter at the post office, Biscuit."
Woof, woof!

"Funny puppy! Come back.
It's not our turn yet."
Woof!

"Here's the pet shop, Biscuit.
You need a new bone and a new ball."
Woof, woof!

"Sit, Biscuit, sit. Mind your manners, silly puppy!
Now Mr. Brown will give you a biscuit.
Thank you, Mr. Brown."
Woof!

"Come along, Biscuit.
It's time to visit the library.
We can return this book and choose
another book to borrow.
We can listen to a story, too."

Woof, woof! Woof, woof!
"*Sshhh!* Quiet, Biscuit!
That's too loud for inside the library."
Woof!

"The florist is next on Mom's list.
This plant is just right for our garden."
Woof, woof!

"Oh, no, Biscuit. No digging!"
Woof!

"We must help clean up.
That's the way, Biscuit."

"We're almost finished with our errands, Biscuit.
We need bread, eggs, and bananas from the market."
Woof, woof!

"Good puppy!
You can carry a bag, too."
Woof!

"Look, Biscuit!
Our friends are at the ice cream shop!
What shall we have?"
Woof, woof!

"Sweet puppy!
You found a tasty treat to share with Puddles."
Bow wow!
Woof!

"It's time to go home, Biscuit.
Our walk was a lot of fun."
Woof, woof!

"Helping with errands is lots of fun, too,
especially with a sweet puppy like you!"
Woof!

Say hello, Biscuit!
Woof, woof!
Biscuit greets others in his special way.
Draw a circle around the words that we say when
we greet people. Draw a square around the words
we say when it's time to leave.

Hello

Bye

How are you?

Good-bye

I'm pleased to meet you.

It was nice seeing you.

See you soon!

Hi

To see the answer, turn to the last page.

Wait your turn, Biscuit!
Biscuit must learn to be patient.
What treat is there for Biscuit when he waits his turn?
Help Biscuit through the maze to find out.

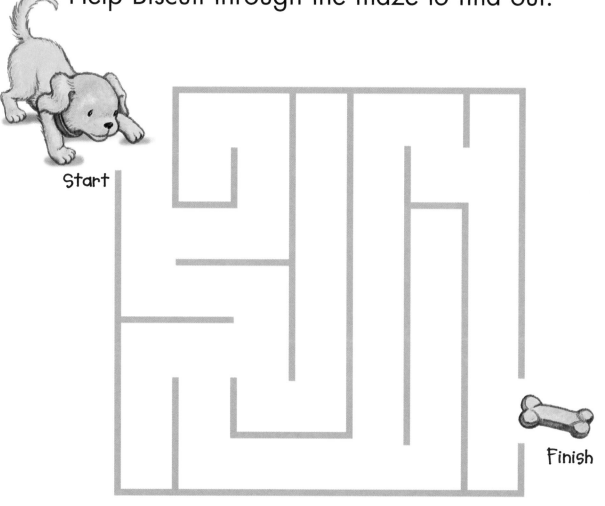

Start

Finish

To see the answer, turn to the last page.

Sometimes we must use voices that are quiet.
Sometimes we can use voices that are loud.
Draw a blue circle around places where we should use a quiet voice, or an inside voice.
Draw a red circle around places we can use a loud voice, or our outside voice.

To see the answer, turn to the last page.

Biscuit likes to share a bone
with his friend Puddles.
What do you like to share with your friends?
Draw a picture of things you like to share.

It's fun to help, Biscuit!
Biscuit knows lots of ways to help.
What are some ways that you like to help?

I can help by

Help Biscuit unscramble these letters
to find words that help us to be polite.

spalee

hantk ouy

m'l rrosy

csueex em

ouy'er elcmowe

To see the answer, turn to the last page.

ANSWER KEY

Say hello, Biscuit!

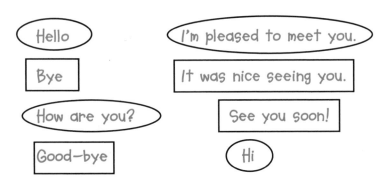

(Hello)

[Bye]

(How are you?)

[Good-bye]

(I'm pleased to meet you.)

[It was nice seeing you.]

[See you soon!]

(Hi)

Wait your turn, Biscuit!

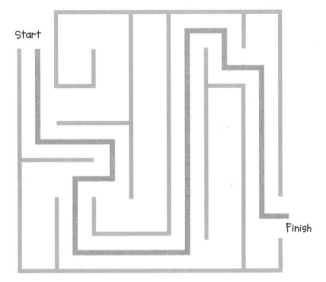

Start

Finish

Quiet in the library, Biscuit!

Mind your manners, Biscuit!

please

thank you

I'm sorry

excuse me

you're welcome